Covenant
of Lies
The Revealed Truth

By Holly Spence

Purchase Monarch Publications, LLC books in
bulk for educational, business, fundraising, or
sales promotional use. For more information,
please email monarchpublicationsllc@yahoo.com

Spence, Holly 2010
Covenant of Lies the Revealed Truth/ By Holly
Spence

ISBN-10: 0578065819
ISBN-13: 978-0578065816

Front and back cover designed by Timothy Hawkins

Well….this is the second release in the "Covent of Lies" series. I can hardly believe that I have published four books and two stage productions. God is AWESOME! It is HIS grace upon my life!

Thank you for showing your support by purchasing my books. Please enjoy and send your feedback to monarchpublicationsllc@yahoo.com

Holly Spence

Table of Contents

About the Author

With a passion to know, learn and live God's Word. My wife has been anointed by God to deliver His Word to His people.

A native of Cincinnati, Ohio, Holly Spence is a graduate of the School for Creative and Performing Arts in which she majored in Drama, Technical Theater Management and Vocal Music. She attended the University of Cincinnati, majoring in Chemical Technology. She currently serves as an OU Americas Sales LVC Program Manager for Oracle Corporation.

She is a literary award nominated author and playwright *("Servant Leadership The Heart That Serves" & "Power of 10 Gaining Empowerment in 10 minutes, 10 words, 10 people", "STOP! You're Killing", "Covenant of Lies the Untold Truth" and "Covenant of Lies the Revealed Truth*), Conference Speaker and Workshop Facilitator. She was nominated as 2009 Female Author of the Year for the AAMBC Awards of San Antonio, Texas and Monarch Publications, LLC her publishing company as Publisher of the year.

My wife has a true servant's heart; she is committed to covenant relationships and has a passion for God's Word. She is a covenant member of Overflow Ministries Covenant Church where she submits and serves under the Godly government of Apostle Bennie and Pastor Delores Fluellen. She is an anointed psalmist, entrepreneur, and businessperson. She is the mother of three beautiful children Heather, Jehoshua, and Joshijah-rapha. She is my best friend and covenant partner.

Vinnie C. Spence

Acknowledgements

"Covenant Lies The Revealed Truth" is the sequel to Covenant Lies The Untold Truth. This is the second installment of the "Covenant of Lies" trilogy series.

To my editor and critic, my hermana, Melissa Allen. Thank you for your continued support and encouragement.

To one of my best friends, Cira Law we have been brought back together for such a time as this. Thanks for jumping in on this project and lending your expertise as only you can. Love you girl!

To authoress K. Lyn Brown – "Control Issues" and Rebecca Campbell-Greene "Sisters In The Name of Love" and "Diary 15" series. Your glowing reviews were a definite fuel of encouragement. Rebecca thank you for your review of the complete series, I thank God for our connection.

To Mrs. Anita M. Boclair, Founder of B.R.A.N.C.H.E.S of Bookclub, your tireless efforts and support I appreciate. *"Thank you"* just doesn't seem to be enough. You are an agent of every author's wish.

Timothy Hawkins, your work continues to make me proud son!

Dad and Mom (Apostle Bennie and Pastor Delores Fluellen), thanks for your continued support and love. Keep doing what you do and giving us permission, through your example to operate in my grace.

To my brother Pastor Michael A. Rucker there is *"Seed – Time – and Harvest"* now there is *"Put the Shut to the Up"*. I am about my Father's business.

To my sister, Joy Strong, who is credited with naming the "Covenant of Lies" series and responsible for editing this book as well. Thank you Joy, for your love, support and promotion of the series. Your name is in the book!

To my mother, Winona Strong, Are you still crying? Did you ever think? I am simply amazed… tell me later or write in down so you don't cry.

To my children Heather, Jehoshua and Joshijah-rapha, Joshijah the first published author in the family. Joshijah continue to work on your second project. Heather and Jehoshua we are STILL waiting for the two of you!

To my covenant partner, Vinnie Spence, I love you! Thank you for your continued support of all my ideas…you never know what God will give me next.

<u>Chapter One</u>

Courtney wakes up, her head is pounding and
blood is all over her lab coat. She does not know
how long she has been out, but she remembers
being knocked out by Calvin Taylor. She looks at
Selma's bed and she is still sleep. Selma was
administered a heavy dose of Percocet to help her
sleep through the night as comfortable as possible.
Courtney then began to look around for Marcie,
calling her by name, but unable to move swiftly.
Water in the bathroom is running. Courtney
managed to get to her knees and use the couch to
get to her feet. When Courtney opened the

1

bathroom door, Marcie was in the shallow shower with water running, bruises on her arms and legs. Her shirt was around her neck; her bra ripped off, her pants and underwear, all at her ankles.

"Oh God!!! Marcie!" Marcie doesn't reply nor does she move. Courtney turns off the water, runs outside for help. The officer was getting up off the floor the same time Courtney was coming out of Selma's hospital room. "Sir, are you ok? I will have someone come by to look at you, don't get up stay seated."

Courtney made her way to the nurse's station, the nurse looked up, "Oh Courtney, what in the world happened?" said the nurse.

"I was attacked by Calvin Taylor, Selma Taylor's husband, please call hospital security and have them dispatch the police. I need to call down regarding my shift, I was supposed to report to work, what time is it?" Courtney sees the clock,

"Oh no, I have been out for over 30 minutes? I also need someone to look at the officer outside Mrs. Taylor's room and I need help getting Marcie Taylor to emergency for examination."

The sixth floor nurse scrambles to meet the request and makes the necessary calls. A second nurse joins Courtney to check out the officer. Courtney heads back down to Marcie with a gown and blankets in hand to cover Marcie. When Courtney gets back to the room, the nurse behind her tends to the officer to identify his injuries. Courtney opens the door. Marcie is still in the bathroom lying in the shower.

"Marcie, I am going to take you to emergency to have you examined." Marcie was still unresponsive. "Marcie, let me help you up, I have a gown for you to put on." Marcie allowed Courtney to help her up, remove her clothing and put the gown and blanket around her.

Just then, John Cartwright arrived from emergency, "Hey Court, I have a wheelchair."

"Thanks John, can you get me a plastic bag? I will need that for her clothes. Come on Marcie, let's get you into the wheelchair, we will get you cleaned up."

John comes back with the plastic bag, as Courtney is lifting Marcie; John places the plastic bag over the back of the wheel chair and proceeds to help Courtney get Marcie into the wheelchair. Just as John reaches out to Marcie, Marcie is like a wild boar, kicking and screaming. Marcie kicks John in his groin; she punches Courtney in her face. Courtney makes every effort to get Marcie to calm down, "John go out," shouted Courtney. When John left the bathroom, Marcie calmed down and Courtney was able to get her into the wheelchair.

During all of this commotion, Selma never woke up. Courtney wheeled Marcie to emergency and called ahead, "Hello this is Nurse Courtney Thomas, I am coming down from the sixth floor and I have a possible rape victim."

Chapter Two

Shane is walking from the Richardson's home on cloud nine, whistling and kicking small rocks on the sidewalk. Shane was surprised by his Aunt Jess' response, so he really didn't know how his parents were going to react, but he was so elated, it didn't matter.

Shane ran up the driveway, turning flips displaying his skills as a gymnast. Shane's exuberance was evident as he entered the code on the front door keypad. Shane continued his flipping routine inside the foyer. Unfortunately, for Shane, his mother was coming down the right side of the staircase.

"SHANE HENRY MCFINLEY! Have you lost your mind? Flipping in my house? You are not too old to get a…" Shane interrupts his mother, when he runs up and picks her up and carries her down the rest of the steps. Stephanie not a heavy women, but like some women was not comfortable when suddenly she was picked up, usually because of the lack of control.
"…SHANE, BOY PUT ME DOWN! What is wrong with you?"

"Mother, its love…" said Shane.
 "There is not that much love in the world for you to pick me up and scaring me half to death!"

Shane carried Stephanie into the great room. Stephanie proceeded into the kitchen and Shane followed.

"So, talk to me about this so called love," said Stephanie. She has a smile on her face because she suspects that Jill is the object of his affection.

"Mom, I finally told her how I feel. It has been exhilarating and freeing. To be able to express my inward feelings and not being rejected helps also..." Shane laughs.

"Who is the young lady that has captured my son's heart?" "Mom! Who else?"
"I don't know mothers are always the last to know anything!" Stephanie smiled. Shane gave her a look of disbelief.

"I knew it! I tried to tell your father, he acted as if I was growing another head."
"I know when I talked to Dad…"
"See proves my point; I am the last to know! What happened when you talked to your dad?" Stephanie hits Shane on his shoulder. She turns and opens the refrigerator to get a bottle of XXX

Pomegranate Vitamin Water. "…he acted as if he was trying to talk me out of it. Mom, I have never been this sure of something. Jill is to be my wife."

"WOW! I knew there was something there, but I definitely didn't know that it was to that extent."
"Yes, ma'am it is. I have already talked to Uncle Carl and Aunt Jess."
"Really!!!? What was the response?"
"Uncle Carl said the same thing you did, *"I knew it!"* Aunt Jess on the other hand surprised me like Dad did." "Okay what did she say?"

"She went into that whole *"what about school thing..."* Mom, we are going to finish school! I am not going to marry her tomorrow, but I want to build the relationship to that end. I thought everyone would be excited for us. I was wrong. I will confess I didn't think you would take it this well."

"What? You didn't, why?" said Stephanie.

"Because I thought you would have some kind of *woman, mother - son thing*…you know…"

"I think you'd better stop while you are ahead. You have some learning to do, don't pull that out on Jill or you will find yourself not in her good graces!" Shane and Stephanie laugh. "Son, I am happy for you!"

Henry walked into the kitchen, "What are we so happy for?"

<u>Chapter Three</u>

Mrs. Perry was getting restless and uncomfortable in her bed. This was new for Gertrude Perry. She was very much used to being independent, moving and getting around the way she wanted. However, her discomfort didn't lead to her calling the nurses or scream in frustration, but it gave her a song in her heart. Most people of Higher Calling didn't know that Mrs. Perry was a recording artist in her late twenties. Her husband was her manager and accompanist. She had the most beautiful, melodious and pitch perfect voice. Mrs. Perry was still struggling to talk but she began to express a heart-felt song.

"When peace, like a river, attendeth my way,
When sorrows like sea billows roll;
Whatever my lot, Thou has taught me to say,
It is well, it is well, with my soul…"

By this time, Mrs. Perry's on duty nurse was standing by the door. She listened as Mrs. Perry continued to sing.

"…Though Satan should buffet, though trials should come,
Let this blest assurance control,
That Christ has regarded my helpless estate,
And hath shed His own blood for my soul.

My sin, oh, the bliss of this glorious thought!
My sin, not in part but the whole,
Is nailed to the cross, and I bear it no more,
Praise the Lord, praise the Lord, O my soul!…"

The melodic sound filled the entire hospital floor. All the nurses and doctors that were on Mrs. Perry's floor were now standing at her door. All of them stood silently, with tears cascading down their faces, regardless of gender. Her song was becoming her musical testament of her relationship with God. Mrs. Perry's voice was so captivating, if you hadn't read her chart you wouldn't have known that she was paralyzed from the waist down after having a severe stroke. Mrs. Perry continues in song.

> *"...For me, be it Christ, be it Christ hence to live:*
> *If Jordan above me shall roll,*
> *No pang shall be mine, for in death as in life*
> *Thou wilt whisper Thy peace to my soul.*
>
> *But, Lord, 'tis for Thee, for Thy coming we wait,*
> *The sky, not the grave, is our goal;*
> *Oh, trump of the angel! Oh, voice of the Lord!*
> *Blessed hope, blessed rest of my soul!*

And Lord, haste the day when my faith shall be
sight,
The clouds be rolled back as a scroll;
The trump shall resound, and the Lord shall
descend,
Even so, it is well with my soul.

It is well...,

with my soul...,"

Mrs. Perry sang the refrain with such a heart-felt conviction. The first "*it is well*" was as if she was keeping time to a bell tower striking the hour. She slowed down as if she was looking into the face of Jesus; she finished the song with musical annotations that obviously naturally gifted.
"...It is well..., it is well..., with my soul.........."[i]

With a smile on her face, Mrs. Perry closed her eyes and fell asleep. Her monitor hummed a flat line.

Chapter Four

Courtney stayed at Marcie's side, entering from the back entrance of the emergency room of the hospital. She was instructing the other nurses in the emergency room what she needed the moment she arrived. John was behind her, also insisting that she get looked at as well. It appeared Courtney suffered one heck of a punch to the nose.

"WOW! Court, have you seen your eye?" Courtney did not notice that her right eye was getting black. She had disregarded her own pain to help an already downtrodden Marcie. Courtney called for a rape kit for Marcie. John called for a cold compress for Courtney.

"Courtney you have to let someone take a look you at you!"
"I will John, I am fine…I have to get this done."
Courtney closed the door to work on Marcie. Courtney talked Marcie through the whole process. When Courtney touched Marcie's legs, it was the second outward expression of emotion from Marcie.

"No, no, no…oh…" tears began to fall, Courtney continued to talk Marcie through the process as she performed the necessary task for the kit.

Chapter Five

The room was still, Jill stood in the middle of her mother's office floor utterly stunned. *Could she have heard what she thought from her mother?* She dared not asked her again; she didn't have the strength or the courage to continue in conversation with her mother. Jill didn't know who, or why? The only thing she did know was her birthday or was that a lie too?

There was a deafening silence in the office between Jessica and Jill. Jessica continued to stand dithering in place and Jill looked at her mother dismayed by her recent announcement. *"He's Your Brother!"* is ringing in Jill's ear.

What Jessica had avoided for years has arrived to force her to reveal truth among her established covenant relationships. It was not Jessica's heart did not care to reveal this truth in such a distressing manner, the fact of the matter was her grandmother's words rang ever so true in this moment *"No need to lie, because the truth is bad enough."*

Jessica stood gazing at Jill with her hand over her mouth, shaking from head to toe, not believing that she had just devastated her daughter with three words. Jessica reached out to Jill as if that would take her words back. As a rushing wind from a category six storm, Jill raised her hand and slapped her mother in the face. Her father was standing in the doorway, "JILL WHAT HAS GOTTEN INTO YOU?!!!" Now crying

18

hysterically and running from the room Jill said,

"Daddy, you have to talk to your wife about that!"

Chapter Six

Marcie curled into a fetal position as Courtney finished her examination. Marcie's experience with the feeling of being dirty, embarrassed and prostituted was one that she had not grown accustomed to. Her father's daily drunken stupors always brought about uncertainty for Marcie. Her bedroom, on many nights, became a den of defiled pleasures for the person that she once looked to for protection and guidance. Now, Marcie's once private suffering has become a public display and she could no longer hide. Mortified by her thoughts, Marcie's begins to have a queasy feeling. She begins to motion for Courtney but she is too late, Marcie's stomach contents were on the floor. Courtney rushed to Marcie with a receptacle. Courtney was concerned with Marcie's regurgitation since she had not eaten much over the past two days. This would be something she would definitely monitor. Courtney immediately ordered an I.V. for anti-dehydration for Marcie.

Marcie's small emergency room quickly filled to capacity; personnel for clean up, another nurse to administer the I.V. and Courtney sitting on the edge of the bed with Marcie. John was still standing at the door ensuring Courtney was not going to be overlooked. Courtney's eye was getting worse with a ring forming around the entire eye.

Marcie rested her head on Courtney's shoulder. Without warning, Marcie began to pour her heart out. "A year and half ago, my life took a turn that I would have never imagined it would. My secure, nurturing, fun loving home turned into an unstable, unpredictable place of repulsion. Church and school became my place of escape outside the lake that sits along the edge of our property at Manor Hill. One decision I was able to make was to drown myself academically. That was one area of my life where I had complete control. I excelled and pushed myself, it gave me a sense of worth and self-confidence. Courtney I am tired of living this life of hell. I have experienced a good life in the past and I know this is not it!"

Courtney listened intently and was glad to hear Marcie opening up. Marcie continued sharing her heart,

"It was a Thursday evening and I came home from a running meet. My mother and father were in the great room. My father was sitting with his head hung low. My mom was kneeling at my father's feet, just rubbing his head and telling him *"It's going to be okay, we will be fine."* I asked what was going on, neither one of my parents replied. I asked my father what was wrong, still nothing. My mother asked him to tell me what was going on. Out of nowhere, my father knocked my mother to the floor and repeatedly kicked her. I tried to stop him and I went flying across the room. When I came to, my mother was holding me, asking if I was okay. This was the first of my father's evil alter ego trips I experienced. That evening I was subjected further to his acts of debauchery. I am so embarrassed and full of shame, but I have to move forward with my life. I don't want to be the cause of the split of my family... but my father has taken advantage of me for the last time."

This is what Courtney was waiting to hear. "Marcie, you have just made a step in the right direction for a better life, I will have a police officer come in."

Chapter Seven

Jill runs out of the room, Carl follows and calls after her.

"Jill, Jill, what is going on?" Jill who has never been a disrespectful child, not even in her early teenage years turns and runs into her father's arms.

"Jill honey, what is it?" said Carl. Jill was too distraught to talk she was beginning to hyperventilate. Carl looked into Jill's eyes and said, "Honey, I have no idea what is going on, but look at me....no matter what, we are going to get through this! Do you hear me Jill? Calm down, no matter what baby, Daddy is here and we will get through this." Jill began to gain her composure as she internalized his words of support.

Carl could not image what had thrown Jill into such a range of emotions; he had to get back to Jessica to find out how an evening that should have been filled with excitement and exuberance, was ending in frenzy and tears. Carl tried to get Jill to come to the office with him.

Jill pleaded, "Please Daddy, I can't… not right now. You and Mom need to talk first anyway; I have to take a back seat to this." Jill kissed her daddy and ran to her room sniffing and crying.

Carl was further perplexed by Jill's last statement. Even in such a devastating moment, Jill was still able to respond maturely setting her own agenda aside. Carl walked back to the office and there

Jessica sat in the middle of the floor with her knees to her chest rocking.

Carl didn't waste time, "Jessica what is going on?" What did you say that caused your normally mature, respectable daughter to slap you in the face as if you were a home invader?"

Jessica continued to rock and cry, "Jessica! Answer me what did you say to Jill?"

Jessica still rocking looked up at Carl and said, "I am so sorry, honey, I am so sorry....please, please forgive me." Carl sat down next to Jessica,

"Honey, forgive you for what?" Jessica grabbed Carl and cried uncontrollably. Carl put his arm around Jessica trying to console her, but he wanted answers. The most important women in his life were both falling apart and he didn't know why. Carl continued to query Jessica about the current state of calamity in his home.

"Jessica, I need you to gather yourself. What are you apologizing for?"

Jessica held on to Carl, she squeezed him and said, "Carl, you know I love you…right?"
Carl replied "Yes."
"We have been through some rough times, but we made it through. Especially early on, our financial issues, our inability to communicate and even through your affair with Beverly Martinez which came much later: but we had already been through so much, the years invested were worth working out…"

Carl was trying not to lose his patience with Jessica, especially since whatever she had to say was definitely difficult for her to reveal, but he really wanted to know the bottom line. Jessica continued,

"…it was during those early years that…" Jessica broke down again in tears. Carl urged her to continue. Jessica proceeded, "…it was during those early years, that we both made bad decisions that were detrimental to ourselves and our relationship..."

Carl perceived what Jessica was going to share, but he was trying to ascertain what that had to do with Jill and the events of tonight. Jill was not aware of the Beverly Martinez affair over five years ago, she was aware that the early years of marriage were rocky, but she didn't have any idea of the details. Jessica continued, "...Carl I had an affair."

Carl had already considered that was the issue and said, "Jessica okay, we can work on that, you have been this route before with me…"

Jessica still shaking all over took long deep breaths just trying to reveal, the total truth to Carl.

Jessica had been operating in her private struggle of untruth for so long that she thought, *"If I do not come right out and say it I will never say it."* Jessica interrupted Carl, "Honey, it's a little different this time. I had an affair and Jill is not your daughter."

Chapter Eight

"Henry your son has come to a very important cross road in his life and he is ready to… well Shane you tell him!" Henry moved toward the refrigerator and pulled out fruit punch Gatorade. "Tell me what?" said Henry. Shane sat on the bar stool under the island.

"Dad we have already talked. You know how I feel about Jill…"
Henry chimes in short and sweet as he sips on his Gatorade. "Yep, we talked!"

"…I had a talk with Uncle Carl and Aunt Jessica tonight and asked their permission regarding my intentions toward Jill."

Henry not surprised but cautious said, "How did Jill handle all of this?"
"Dad, unlike your previous thoughts, Jill was shocked but she was very receptive to the idea," Shane said with the biggest grin.

"Son, I told you your happiness is my biggest concern. Just take it slow, don't rush into anything and don't feel pressured…" Shane cuts his dad off with laughter,

"What is it with you and Aunt Jessica; I don't know who she was tonight. I have never seen her like this. Dad you are not as bad as Aunt Jessica, but you both act as if you don't want us to be together."

"I don't understand it either son, maybe we will understand this one by and by…." Stephanie looked at Henry with a smirk on her face.

Henry replied with his own facial smirk to Stephanie and then addressed Shane, "Son, as a parent I am responsible to guide you…assist you with making decisions that will be beneficial for your future and destiny."

"Dad, we have had this talk before, I know in choosing a wife, we together have to be equally yoked to accomplish our individual and corporate purpose in the earth. Two is always better than one and I know the RIGHT one, you taught me well Dad."

Henry did not say a word; he stood up and hugged Shane. Henry could not avoid this any longer and there was no need. He knew he needed to talk with Stephanie. Shane wrapped his arms around his dad with the same silence.

Stephanie admiring the love between father and son said, "Son, are you ready for school tomorrow? I know this has been one heck of a day, but you do have school!"

"Yes Mom, I have homework I need to knock out." Shane left the kitchen but not before shadow boxing with his dad. Once Shane left the room, Henry took Stephanie by her hand and pulled her close to him by her waist.

"Stephanie McFinley, I love you! You have hung in there with me for richer or poorer, good decisions and bad decisions, truth and lies…..you are still here!"

Stephanie just looked at Henry wondering, where all is this was going. Only Stephanie's time with the Lord would prepare her for what was coming next.

Chapter Nine

Jill lay across her four-post custom bed crying her eyes out. Her shelf of childhood stuffed animals, family pictures and several pictures of her and Shane, were witnessing her cries. Jill's normal bright and luminous room was filled with grief and sorrow. Her DK comforter set, custom bedroom suit and leather bond grouping for her sitting area couldn't erase the sadness in Jill's heart.

How could her best friend, the one that had just expressed his desire to make her his wife be her brother? Jill didn't have the opportunity to ask the most important question, how was Shane her brother? Were they adopted? On the other hand, was Uncle Carl her father? Or was Shane my Dad's son? Nothing was making sense to Jill; it just caused her to cry hysterically.

Jill even in this time of uncertainty was able to cry out in prayer to God. *"Father help me; help me get through this..."* Jill wanted so much to call Shane, but she didn't know what to tell him. She knew the news that *she was his sister* should not come from her but she didn't think it was fair that she was forced to bear this burden alone. There was no one she could turn to, Granny P was in the hospital and her dad was talking with her mom.

When Jill thought about her mother, her tears began to turn to anger. *"How could my mom do this to me?"* The feeling of betrayal was flooding Jill's mind. It caused her breathing to become irregular, she walked back and forth across the floor in her room. Then Jill began to ponder, *"Did my father know? What exactly is the truth?"*

Jill knew that asking these questions of herself wasn't going to get her the desired answers she needed. Only her mother could answer all the questions she had.

As much as Jill wanted answers, she didn't know if she could face her mother. In that instance, it just sank in with Jill that she had left the room after slapping her mother. Jill recognized in that moment that her mother knew she was wrong for lying to her.

Jill's parents had always talked about covenant; keeping covenant, covenant relationships and now these thoughts stoked Jill's anger even more. She said, "All of this talk of keeping covenant and covenant relationships has been nothing but a covenant of lies."

Chapter Ten

Carl sat in the floor of his wife's office in shock.
He slowly removed his arms from around Jessica.
Carl just stared at the wall trying to comprehend
what had just occurred. His beautiful Jill, the one
that he put on his chest to console, the one whose
nose he has wiped, who he taught to ride a bike,
the one he tucked in night after night, the skinned
knees he has kissed and the one he has personally
nurtured into a responsible young lady was not the
seed of his loin. Carl was numb not knowing what
to think or say. He had questions, but could he

handle the answers? This was a deposition he wasn't looking forward to performing.

Carl has made a name for himself as a lawyer; he was a skilled cross-examiner that could break the strongest witness. However, he never had a personal stake in the witness as he does now with Jessica.

Jessica still shaking from head to toe wrapped her arms around Carl hoping that he would not walk out on her. Carl rubbed his hands over his face and up his head, took one deep breath, and exhaled. Nothing could prepare Carl for the line of questioning he was going to let loose on Jessica.

Carl knowing he heard Jessica correctly said, "Jessica, What did you say? Did you say Jill is not my daughter?"

Jessica in fear and trembling replied, "Yes, I don't think she is."

Carl placed his fingertips above his eyebrows and shook his head back and forth in disbelief. This was a difficult situation for Carl to deal with. He didn't struggle so much with Jill not being his seed, because he'd decided right there it didn't matter, Jill was his child and always would be, but the fact that his wife of twenty-one years, his covenant partner would keep such a truth from him was hard to ingest.

Carl always tries not to go into esquire mode on his family, but this situation was yanking the lawyer out of him. "Jessica, I obviously know how long ago this affair was, but who was it with?"

Jessica trying to hold Carl once again said, "Honey, I am so sorry! I know I should have told you, there were so many times, so many things that have happened over the years that I wanted to tell you. I never had the courage and over the past couple of days…."

Carl licking and massaging his lips while Jessica was talking, he was trying to prevent the tears from falling, but to no avail.

Jessica still crying uncontrollably said, "…God has given me opportunity after opportunity to tell you, I didn't want it to come out like this Carl, I am sorry honey, can you forgive me?"

Carl still with much patience considering the situation listened to his wife, but she still failed to answer the question. "Jessica, you still have not answered the question, who is Jill's biological father? And does the man know?"

Jessica nodded and replied, "Yes he knows and he has tried to get me to confront you some time ago and I wouldn't listen. Carl it was a bad decision, we were having problems, it just happened one time…one time only. I couldn't believe it… the one time I was unfaithful I became pregnant. Honey, I am so sorry I am…"

Carl losing his temper cut Jessica off. "JESSICA! Answer the question who is he?"

Jessica shamefully said, "Henry…Henry McFinley."

Chapter Eleven

Courtney sat with Marcie as she completed giving the officer all of the details of her year and a half ordeal with her father. Through all the pain and hurt Marcie made it through, fighting the entire time the spirit of shame and embarrassment. With each question and explanation, Marcie relived the events of her father's sexual abuse.

Mentally and physically drained, Marcie told Courtney, "I feel like a weight has been lifted from my shoulders. Although, I do not know what the future is going to hold, I believe that it can only get better. Courtney do you know what has ultimately gotten me through this?"

Courtney said, "No, what?"

Marcie smiled, "As I look back, it was God. There were times I didn't know if I was going to make it, but I stood on the Word of God, *that all things work together for the good of them that love the Lord and called according to his purpose.* I felt hopeless and wanted to give up many times, but in this moment, I have come to realize that God has kept me for a purpose. I will fulfill that purpose even though I don't understand it all."

Courtney's eyes filled with tears; she had walked away from God years ago. Frustrated and mad at God for taking her mother when she did not have the courage to try stopping the abuse. Courtney realized listening to Marcie, if Marcie could be brave enough to make changes in her life, she could be brave enough to ask God for forgiveness and come back to Him.

"Marcie, I have been so angry with God and blaming Him for my plight in life that I walked away from Him. Your courage today gives me the courage to go back to Him humbly and ask for forgiveness."

Marcie with the biggest smile on her face said, "I am fulfilling my purpose already. God is faithful, even to a seventeen year old girl."

John knocked on the door, "Hey ladies, how are we doing?" John saw the tears and smiles, "Everything okay?"

Marcie chimed in with much joy "Sure is! Courtney just gave her heart back to the Lord! John, do you know the Lord Jesus Christ as your savior?"

John's eyes almost jumped out of his head and he began to jump straight up and down in the air saying "Thank you Jesus! Thank you Jesus!" Courtney and Marcie were both shocked, Marcie said, "Wow, I wasn't expecting that response, but I will take it!"

John explained, "Courtney I have been praying for you since we met four years ago and I am excited that God answers prayer!" John grabbed Courtney hugging and rocking with her back and forth on the bed.

Courtney said, "OKAY, John, I didn't even know you were saved, well now that I think about it…there was something definitely different about you…now I know what it was. Thank you for praying for me, thank you both. Now I feel like a weight has been lifted off my shoulders."

The three of them continued to talk, laugh and share. John was still elated and jumping on the inside. Part of John's prayer was answered, he was so excited he wanted to share the other part of his prayer, but he knew that was a little too much, so he kept that to himself for now, waiting for the appropriate time.

Courtney said, "Marcie, let me get you processed and ready to go upstairs. We can put another bed in your mom's room, if there are no objections." Marcie started to reply, but instead she became sick at the stomach again and grabbed the trash receptacle to catch her stomach contents. John ran out to get more towels.

"Marcie you'd better lay down!" said Courtney.

Chapter Twelve

Shane, after running up the staircase, continues jogging to his room and jumps on his king size bed. Shane lay with his arms behind his head, *"If I knew that I would feel this good, I would have told Jill a long time ago about my feelings for her....oh well, all in time."*

Shane grabbed his cordless phone from his nightstand and dialed Jill at home. The phone rang with no answer. Shane did not need to double check the number because he and Jill have tied up the line since junior high school, so their parents agreed to install private lines for the both of them in their rooms. Shane started to call again, but decided he would get his things together for tomorrow and knock out his homework real quick.

Henry was holding Stephanie in his arms, when she said, "Henry, I love you too! And yes I am still here and I don't plan on leaving."

Henry began to cry. Stephanie surprisingly was not moved much by the tears. She kept whispering a prayer to God that she would not react in her emotions and that she would hear from God concerning her marriage. This whole issue with Jill and Shane obviously was stirring up something that she was not aware of. Stephanie was bracing herself for what was going to come next. Stephanie wiped the tears from Henry's eyes with her thumbs.

"Henry, babe we agreed early on that communication and openness was the second key to our successful marriage after God, so what do you need to say?"

Henry laying his head on Stephanie's forehead and holding her even tighter said,

"I know and this is something I should have shared with you long ago, I..." Henry was interrupted by the doorbell. Henry took a deep breath and said, "I will be right back."

Stephanie said, "Who could it be this hour of the night?" Henry shuffled through to the foyer wiping his tears and put on his game face to answer the door. Henry opened the front door. With much force and less warning Carl stepped through the door and punched Henry so hard he fell back and slid across the marble floor. Carl walked right to him and continued throwing as many punches as he possibly could. All the punches were thrown without one word. All that could be heard was the commotion of Carl coming through the door and the contact of each one of his punches on Henry.

Stephanie came running from the kitchen when she reached the foyer, she screamed, "CARL STOP IT! WHAT IS WRONG WITH YOU?"

By this time, Shane was at the top of the steps watching his Uncle Carl beat on his father. Henry was lying on the floor trying to block each punch, but not defending himself. When Carl heard Stephanie's voice, he retreated from beating Henry senseless as if he was in a back alley brawl in Miami.

Stephanie knowing there was a cause still asked Carl again, "WHAT HAS GOTTEN INTO YOU? DO YOU REALLY HAVE TO RESORT TO THIS?"

Carl simply and calmly replied, "Ask your husband." Carl turned and walked out the door.

Chapter Thirteen

Jill having ignored her phone ringing did not even look at the caller ID, she was more concerned with why the front door slammed, she called out to her dad, but there was no response. She went downstairs to his office and then looked in his bedroom he wasn't there.

Jill ran back up to her mother's office, the door was wide open the office had papers and books everywhere. It appeared the office had been ransacked. She had never seen any part of the house look like this not even when they were moving.

Jill called out again, "Daddy?" no answer and no movement in the office and she called again, "Mommy?" no answer. Jill then heard someone come in the door. "Daddy?"

The phone rang, "Richardson residence, yes….she is not available…Oh Lord no! When? Okay thank you for calling." Carl hung up the phone, when he turned around, with tears in his eyes; Jill was standing in front of him. "Oh Daddy, I am so sorry!"

Carl said, "Baby girl, don't you worry about me, you will always be daddy's baby." Carl picked Jill up as he had done since she was a little girl. He held and rocked with her as they both cried.

Jill said, "Daddy, are we going to be okay?"

Carl still crying said, "Honey we will always be okay, know that I love you to life! That hasn't and won't change."

Jill replied, "… and you will always be my daddy!"
Carl put Jill down and wiped her tears with the handkerchief he pulled from his pocket. Still holding her in his arms Carl said, "Jill this night has been shocking for the both of us but unfortunately the bad news is still coming…"

Jill did not know how much more she could take tonight. She had already learned that her father wasn't her father and the only thing that could make this worse if her father was Uncle Henry and she thought, *"that's not possible…but it explained alot"* Jill said, "What is it Daddy, you should just go ahead and tell me."

"Honey, Granny P died tonight." Jill let out the loudest scream and fell in her father's arms.

Chapter Fourteen

Shane ran down the steps, "Dad you okay?"
Stephanie went to the kitchen to get some ice. Carl
had tagged Henry good. Henry's nose was
bleeding, possibly broken and he definitely had a
black eye.

Carl replied, "Yes, son I am okay."
"What was that all about with Uncle Carl?"
Stephanie returned with the ice in time to hear the
question.

"Shane, go upstairs Dad and I will come up later."
Shane clearly annoyed but not disrespectful said,
"Mom I am not that six-year-old boy any longer, I
can handle this." Stephanie who was just thinking
of her son's emotional protection conceded and
said okay. While Stephanie did not know for sure
the nature of Carl's outburst, she was very sure
now that Henry's confession was going to be
explosive.

"Okay, son you are right." Stephanie continued to
clean Henry up. She and Shane moved him into
the family room.

Henry holding the bag of ice over his eye and
towel over his nose removed both and said, "I
didn't want….I guess it would have never
mattered, it would have been hard either way, but
earlier better than later would have been the best
decision."

Henry looking at Stephanie and Shane proceeded, "Babe, son….I apologize to both of you. I have broken covenant with you. I have betrayed your trust, love and confidence. Shane let me talk with your Mom alone for a second, man."

Stephanie spoke up and said, "Henry, I am okay. Let Shane stay, he is going to need the both of us for this." Henry looked at Stephanie in disbelief and gratefulness. If Henry had any doubt, he knew in that split second he had a jewel of a wife.

Henry continued, "About eighteen years ago, I stepped out of the marriage covenant. There is no excuse and no justification for my actions. What was or wasn't going on with your mother and me, still doesn't offer an excuse for me breaking covenant…"

Henry took a deep breath; Stephanie grabbed Henry by his hand and shifted next to him on the couch. Henry held his head down and began sobbing. Shane had not seen his father this vulnerable outside of his moments of worship around the house and in church. He was amazed at his mom's response, the lack of anger and the love she was showing toward his father in this minute of declared disloyalty.

Henry continued, "….further salt to the wound is that I had an affair with Jessica…Aunt Jessica…" Now Shane's eyebrows are raised and he is paralyzed in his spot. Stephanie still unmoved just holds Henry's hand tighter. Henry in tears says, "…and Jill is your sister."

Shane jumps up and throws his arm back as if he is going to hit his father but he catches his self and breaks into tears. His parents stand and hug to console him, "Shane I am so sorry man…forgive….please forgive me!" said Henry.

Chapter Fifteen

As John rolled Marcie upstairs, they laughed and talked all the way to the room. Her mother is still asleep. Marcie is glad her mother missed the events of the night. Although this was one of Marcie's most horrible days, she felt better than she had in years. Marcie looked at John with a girly smile and said,

"You were awfully excited about Ms. Courtney…you like her don't you?"
"Well that's getting to the point isn't it? We barely know each other and you want me to share such

intimate details and affairs of my heart." John said all with a smile of guilt. Marcie laughed covering her mouth, trying not to disturb her mother.

"So, when are you going to tell her?" said Marcie.
"WOW, you are not letting up…"
"It's my new found freedom!" Marcie smiled.
"Yes and you ARE free indeed. I haven't told her, I just had one prayer answered I will wait….let me ask her out first."

Marcie with a nod of approval said, "Okay, I will keep checking in with you." They both smiled and chuckled at the other. John walked out of the room.

Marcie was hoping she was going to be able to fall right to sleep. You would think with all that occurred she would fall right off to sleep, but that wasn't so. Marcie felt the over whelming need to pray for her father. Part of her wanted to deny the feeling but felt that she couldn't dare. Marcie immediately began to pray.

<u>Chapter Sixteen</u>

Carl told Jill, "I will go upstairs and tell your mother about Granny P."

"Daddy, I don't know where she is, when I was looking for you I couldn't find her," said Jill through her tears.

"Did you look in the bedroom?"
Jill said, "Yes and in your office before you came in. Her office is a mess that's another reason why I was looking for you."

Carl went to his bedroom, looked in the bathroom and both walk in closets. Carl checked the media room and game room downstairs, there was no Jessica. He checked to make sure the car wasn't gone and it was still parked in the garage. It was just registering with him that Jill said the office was a mess. Carl ran up the stairs he began to call Jessica. No response. He checked all of the rooms upstairs and went back to the office.

The office was just as Jill mentioned a mess; Carl wondered what happened in here after he left. As upset as he was, he knows he did not do this. Jessica wasn't anywhere to be found. Carl went back down stairs to the garage and grabbed a flashlight to look for Jessica in the back yard. At the edge of the property was a little creek. Jessica talked about having a sitting area there. Carl thought maybe she was there. Even in all of his anger, Carl did not want to go to bed without making sure Jessica was at least in the house. He recognized that she was emotionally a wreck and did not know exactly what was running through her head other than shame and embarrassment.

Jill continued to look for her mother the in house. Opening closet doors and calling her name. "Mom where are you?" Jill went back into the office and went to the closet door. When she opened the door, there her mother sat rocking back and forth twirling her hair between her fingers.

Jill ran back down the steps to the back yard, to call for her dad. By the time she got to the deck door, her father was walking back toward the house.

"Daddy, I found her, she doesn't look good at all!" Carl started running toward the house, "Where is she baby girl?"

"She's upstairs in her office…" Carl started walking toward the stairs when Jill continued, "…she's in the closet." Carl stopped and look at Jill with a wrinkled forehead,

"What? The closet?" said Carl

"Yes and she's rocking back and forth twirling her hair with her fingers," said Jill.

Carl thought Jill was right, that's not a good sign. Carl ran up the staircase straight to the office stepping over everything Jessica had thrown on the floor. In the closet, there was Jessica rocking back and forth and twirling her hair with her figures, mumbling words that he didn't understand. Carl reached for Jessica, she continued to rock and mumble not responding to Carl and not responding to his urges to get her out of the closet. Carl attempted to pull her out of the closet but that was a mistake he would not try again. Jessica went crazy beating herself in the head and up against the wall. Carl immediately removed his hands from her and stepped back. Jill was in the office with her hands over her mouth.

"Get me the phone baby girl….get me the phone." Jill moved after the second request. Carl dialed the only person he knew that could help.

Chapter Seventeen

Shane just cried, cried and cried in his dad's arms. "Dad, I love her, I love her so much." Henry didn't know what to say, he just held his son as long as he would allow him to hold him. Stephanie had her small arms around both of her men. She was more concerned with Shane than processing her own feelings.

Shane's cries were deep and loud and then suddenly he just stopped crying as if someone had flipped a switch. He looked at them both and said, "Can I go to my room?"

The phone rang before Stephanie or Henry replied. Stephanie said, "Just one moment let me get the phone…hello, yes…no they didn't…oh wow…okay I will…what? Of course, I will be right there." Stephanie hung up the phone. Stephanie turned and there were tears streaming down her face.

"Mom what's wrong now?"
"Granny P…..she died." Shane having already reached his saturation level fell to his knees and said, "God!!! Enough is enough already, Oh God, Oh God!"

Stephanie and Henry both knelt down with Shane everyone holding each other. Stephanie then said, "I need to go over Carl's…" Shane interrupted in his tear stricken voice, "How is Jill? I know this can't be easy."

"I am not sure, but that was Carl and he said Jessica is not doing well. She is not well at all."

Henry trying to be the brave and protective husband said, "I will go with you." Stephanie very emphatically said, "NO! You stay here, I will be fine."

"Mom let me go with you; I need to check on Jill. "I would be comfortable with that," said Henry.

Shane ran up the staircase to get his shoes. Henry while wiping his tears, Stephanie leaned over and told him, "We are going to make it through this, I love you Henry McFinley and what God has joined together let no man put asunder."

Chapter Eighteen

Mark Swindoll was sitting at his desk in his office. He is filing papers and completing paperwork for his report. Mark decided to go back to the office after leaving the hospital visiting Selma Taylor. Mark met Selma two years ago. Mark and Selma met while serving on the games committee during the annual Higher Calling Covenant Community Festival. Mark was told very often that he was the only person Selma appeared to connect with after she returned to church. That connection was short lived after Cal Taylor returned. The conversations and occasional phone calls between Mark and

Selma were definitely brought to a halt. Selma's behavior turned to absolute fear to even acknowledge Mark's presence. Mark recognized the difference and gave Selma the necessary space she needed.

Mark thought about Selma, he thought about his life over the past two years. He had really grown attached to some of the people at Higher Calling, but Mark wasn't certain that he could remain at Higher Calling if his relationship with Selma was severed. As Mark goes through his mail, he comes across a greeting card that was sent over two weeks ago. Mark removed his letter opener from his drawer and proceeds to open the envelope. Mark reads the card and it brings a smile to his face.

<u>Chapter Nineteen</u>

Shane and Stephanie pull up in front of the Richardson's home as they have many times before. However, this time was unquestionably like no other. So much has occurred over the last twenty-four hours from death to the possibility of her best friend facing a psychotic break. Not to mention this same best friend has slept with her husband who has fathered her child.

Shane turned the key in the ignition, turned to his mom and said, "Mom, you are amazing woman!

When I think about what has just occurred tonight, there is a calmness about you that is almost frightening."

Stephanie smiled at Shane and rubbed her hand across his face. "I know son, I was thinking the same thing riding over. What you see it's *not me, but the Christ in me…to whom much is given, much is required.* I have been forgiven much, so much I have to forgive. I am more concerned about you than me."

Shane returned the smile to his mother and said, "Seeing and hearing you, allow me to witness firsthand the example of Christ. As you always say, how you act gives me permission to behave the same way. Your behavior hasn't given me permission to go off…you are amazing!"

Shane and his mother hugged and Stephanie kissed him and said, "I love you son!"

Stephanie and Shane walk to the front door and ring the doorbell. The eight-ring bell chime can be heard outside.

Carl opens the door and immediately begins apologizing and shows his gratefulness to Stephanie and Shane for coming over. "Stephanie, thank you so much for coming! I am sorry about my earlier display of disappointment. I should have…."

Stephanie interrupts Carl, "Carl I value our relationship more than our circumstance, we can work through this." Carl and Stephanie embrace. Shane looks on still utterly amazed by his mother's strength.

Carl turns and says to Shane, "Shane I would like to apologize to you, that is not how a man should behave or settle his disputes and I hate that you had to witness that." Carl reached out to Shane and they embraced.

Shane replied, "Uncle Carl, completely understandable."

Shane noticed movement out of the corner of his eye from the great room, he saw Jill standing there. He turned to meet her with his eyes; he knew that this vision of beauty wasn't his sister. Right before the phone rang at home, Shane just stopped crying instantly because he was convinced that Jill wasn't his sister. Shane moved swiftly to Jill and hugged her.

Jill feeling a little strange considering the turn of events, held Shane for dear life. As she hugged him, they both begin to cry, Jill thought, "*Shane has gone from my best friend to my boy friend to my brother all in less than twelve hours.*"

Carl and Stephanie walked over to the couple to offer their warm embrace. The four of them, stood there in the foyer crying.

Stephanie wiping her eyes said, "Carl, take me to Jessica." Carl and Stephanie proceeded up the left side of the staircase. Shane and Jill went into the great room.

Shane looked at Jill, "How are you doing…I guess that's a stupid question?"

Jill said, "It's okay, I don't know what to say either…I was thinking while you were holding me, you went from my best friend, to boy friend to brother in a matter seconds it seems."

"Well you can't say our life together hasn't been interesting…" Shane tried to lighten things up.

"Shane you can always make me laugh, even in this crazy situation. So how is Uncle Henry or do I call him Dad? Oh weird!"

"Well after Uncle Carl came over and beat his tail…" Jill interrupted, "WHAT?!"
"…yea, Uncle Carl walked through the door and beat dad like Ali on Frazier. I didn't know whether to try and break it up or start dancing and singing Michael Jackson's Beat It!" Shane fell out laughing on the couch. "Okay, I was wrong for that one…but it sure is funny." Shane and Jill both laughed.

Shane looks at Jill and says, "All kidding aside, we are not brother and sister. After I got over the initial shock of it all, I really felt in my spirit we are not brother and sister."

Jill looked at Shane and said, "I want to believe with you but…."

"Don't worry, I have faith enough for the both of us," said Shane.

Carl walked Stephanie in the office and said, "She's in the closet in here." Stephanie took one look at Jessica and she knew.

"Carl she is suffering a break." Stephanie grabbed her cell phone out of her purse. She called the Rose Farland Wellness Center.

R.F.W.C was a private center that Stephanie previously worked for and with for many years. Stephanie knew it would be critical for Jessica to get there now. "Hi, this is Dr. Stephanie McFinley, please transfer me to the third floor."

"Hello this is Rodney Carter, how may I help you?" Stephanie didn't waste any time with the pleasantries, she got right down to business.

"Hi Rodney, Dr. Stephanie McFinley do you have a private room available?"

"Hello, Dr McFinley, yes, yes we do."

"Please prepare it for Jessica Richardson. I hope to be there within the hour....okay, thank you!"

Stephanie put her cell phone back in her purse and placed her purse on the desk. Stephanie approached the closet with caution. Stephanie's eyes were filled with tears as she sat down in front of the closet door.

"Hi Jessica." Jessica did not reply she did however look at Stephanie. Stephanie extended her hand to Jessica. "Jessica can you come out of the closet?" Jessica just looked at Stephanie twirling her hair. "Jessica come out of the closet, let's take a ride so you can get better and stop feeling the way you do....Jessica it's okay, come on out....Jessica it's Stephanie."

Jessica stopped twirling her hair and stared at Stephanie. Stephanie held her hand out and said, "Jessica it's going to be okay."

Jessica crawled out of the closet and fell in Stephanie's arm and said, "Help me!"

Chapter Twenty

Henry sat on the floor in the family room with his
head between his knees, still holding the ice on his
eye. Carl threw a mean punch; Henry knew he
deserved every hit. He and Carl had been friends
for so long. Not only did he let down his best
friend, he also hurt Stephanie and Shane.

Henry wanted to tell them all before now. Jessica
was the driving force to ensure that it didn't
happen. Henry should not have allowed that to
stop him from making things right.

Henry continued to think about Stephanie and her response to the whole thing. In the middle of his pity party, he could not help but acknowledge what an amazing display of unconditional love Stephanie was showing. He did not know if she was in shock and had not had the opportunity to go through her range of emotions, but for now it was still very impressive.

Shane on the other hand, he had not seen him break down like that since he was a boy falling off his tike bike. He wanted to make it right and gain his trust, faith and respect, but he wondered, *"could Shane ever forgive him?"* He could not imagine what Jill was thinking at this point, Henry wondered if *"...she would even look at him the same way."* He further thought, *"...would Jill blame him for her family break up and the condition her mother was in now?"* Henry has the potential to lose his whole family and those that he considered family all in the same day. Henry fell to the floor and wept like a baby.

Chapter Twenty-one

Stephanie held Jessica in her arms both crying and rocking. Their years of friendship can be seen through each time the two of them rocked back and forth.

Carl stood watching in tears, even through his anger he didn't want to see Jessica in this mental condition. Carl thought, *"Maybe if he hadn't pushed her she wouldn't be in this state."* That feeling went away as a transitory thought; Carl knew, *"this was Jessica's responsibility for the current state of her mental affairs."*

Stephanie knew she needed to get Jessica to Rose Farland Wellness Center. She motioned for Carl to help them up. Stephanie held on to Jessica and said, "Jessica we are going to get you some help. We are going to go to the Rose Farland Wellness Center. I am going to have Carl take us."

Jessica just kept saying, "Help me!"

Stephanie and Carl managed to get Jessica down the staircase. Jill seeing her mother began to cry. Shane put his arm around Jill. Carl said, "Shane will you stay here with Jill until we get back?" "Sure Uncle Carl, no problem."

Stephanie and Carl arrive at Rose Farland; Rodney Carter was at the admittance door with a wheelchair when they pulled up. "Hello Dr. McFinley, I have paperwork prepared for Mr. Richardson to complete at his leisure."

"Rodney thank you so much for your attentiveness," said Stephanie.

Stephanie and Carl put Jessica in the wheelchair. Jessica was still twirling her hair and rocking, she would not let Stephanie's hand go.

Rose Farland's Wellness Center was a state of the art, top notch center for the elite and catered to celebrities around the country. The décor and service was more on the lines of a five star modern chic hotel than a rehab center. Carl was aware of the facility but had never been inside. "Jessica, this is very nice!" said Carl.
"Yes it is, Jessica should be quite comfortable here," said Stephanie.

Once they reached Jessica's room, Jessica started to rock harder and cry, "Help me!" Stephanie told Rodney to prepare a sedative and show Carl to the waiting area. Stephanie proceeded to try to get Jessica to calm down.

"Jess, it's me Stephanie. You are going to stay here for a while. I will be able to help you here." Jessica stopped crying, *"Help me!"* and her rocking was slowing down. Stephanie walked her to the bed and helped her into the navy blue silk pajamas that are provided. Rodney returned and administered the sedative.

Stephanie joined Carl in the waiting room. Stephanie dropped on the leather couch "Whew! This has been a day!"

Carl bending over with his elbows on his knees said, "Yes it has! Stephanie I am sorry again for busting into your home like that. There is no excuse..."
Stephanie nodded an acceptance of his apology.

"...I was so angry and I wouldn't dare hit Jessica. I have such an assortment of emotions. I cannot believe she was unfaithful, I cannot believe she was unfaithful with my best friend and HER best friend's husband; I cannot believe she kept this from me. If nothing else, she should not want to hurt Jill with all of this. So punching Henry was my first release of emotion. How are you doing with all of this?"

Stephanie just as calm replied, "I am actually fine. I love my husband and we are going to work through this. We have too much time invested in one another….for what? to throw it all away. I still believe, that what God joined together twenty years ago he is faithful to complete."

"Stephanie, that sounds good, but you are not the least bit upset? I just can't believe they would..."

Stephanie interrupts Carl. "Carl, lest you forget, it's the mercies of God, it's not us…" Carl looked at Stephanie curiously.

"…I can pin point when this happened. Both of our marriages were in turmoil. You were ready to walk out on Jessica and I was ready to walk out on Henry. You and I have always been able to talk, don't tell me you don't remember that point in time. We almost…"

Carl interrupted, "Yea, I remember and we ALMOST….but Stephanie…WE DIDN'T!"

"Carl, calm down, I know we didn't, but my point is we were there." Carl began to cry; Stephanie walked over to him and hugged him.

While they were embraced, Carl said, "Stephanie thank you, thank you for everything and most importantly for being a good friend!"

"Carl you are welcome! Jessica has been given something to help her sleep. We should get back to Jill and Shane."

Chapter Twenty-two

Courtney was sitting at the nurse's desk with her head in her hands. John approached Courtney, "Hey Court, you doing okay?"

"Hey John, the last twenty-four hours has been no joke." Courtney looked up,

"Whoa, Court you need to keep that ice pack on. I will get one for you."

John returns with the ice pack. John gently puts the pack on Courtney's face, she jumps, "Oh I am sorry Court; you have to take care of yourself that is a good shiner. Have they found Mr. Taylor?"

"No and I haven't heard a thing, and prefer to keep it that way. Do you think you should go home for the night?"
"No John I can't, there is no one to cover for me. I will be okay."
"I will check with you in the next two hours and see if you are ready for a break and we can steal some more time to talk."

Courtney with the icepack on her eye watched John as he walked away. John turned and waved and she returned the favor. Courtney was smitten by John's
attentativeness. Courtney desperately wanted to trust someone. Courtney wondered if her years of loneliness could finally end. She wasn't too hopeful, she was not sure if John would be willing to handle the baggage she carried.

Chapter Twenty-three

Shane and Jill were finished watching their second movie when Jill let out the loudest yawn. "Someone is sleepy, I know it's past your bedtime," Shane laughed.

"Yes it is," replied Jill. "Shane, I don't know about you but this has been a day that I never expected! I never had the opportunity to ask my mother any questions. I was so upset….I actually slapped her…"

"You slapped Aunt Jessica? I wanted to punch my dad but I didn't want to get punched back," laughed Shane.

"...Yes, I slapped her I was in complete shock, to realize my Dad is not my dad. More distressing is that Uncle Henry is my father."

Jill began to cry and Shane just held her in his arms. "Jill, I told you and a DNA test will soon prove it all, we are not brother and sister. I don't feel that we are."

"What do you think will happen to our parents? Will we remain friends and their relationship will dissolve?"

"My mom is taking this so well it's unbelievable. She sat by my father's side as he told the both of us. She is incredible. She is the living example of Christ; she held my father's hand the whole time. Dad on the other hand was a mess while confessing his indiscretion. I haven't seen such tears from him unless he was worshipping."

"Shane, was it one time, several times, what?"

"I don't know," replied Shane.

"Did Aunt Stephanie know?" said Jill.

"NO! I am telling you, you would have to see it to believe it," said Shane.

"Aunt Stephanie has always been the peacemaker; I just don't know what my dad is going to do, if he was angry as you say…."

"Oh, Uncle Carl was pissed!" interrupted Shane.

The door opened from the garage, Carl and Stephanie walked through. They both looked so worn and tattered emotionally and physically. They all exchanged their greetings.

"Daddy, how is mommy?"

"She is resting baby girl."

"Jill, your mom is going to be okay, she just needs some time." Carl sat in the family room.

Stephanie remains standing and says to Shane
"Are you ready?"

"Aunt Stephanie, can we all talk for a moment, I
..." "Absolutely Jill, you don't have to explain
yourself. I will stay as long as you need me to."

"I am just trying to wrap my brain around this,"
said Jill.

Shane chimed in, "I told Jill…I really believe…I
mean I feel it in my spirit we are not brother and
sister."

Carl replied, "Really?"

"Yes, Uncle Carl! Jill doesn't want to get her
hopes up but I told her I will have faith enough for
the both of us."

Stephanie just smiled at Shane and said, "Son, I
will join my faith with yours and believe with
you!" Shane returned the smile to his mother.
Stephanie continued, "I have seen how Shane

cares for you Jill. He desires to have you as his wife and he is a Godly young man. He knows that his faith in God will give him the desires of his heart."

"I told you Jill; no matter what, you will always be baby girl. However, I will schedule a DNA test as soon as possible to start some resolution," said Carl.

Chapter Twenty-four

Stephanie and Shane arrived home, "Mom, my hero…" Shane and Stephanie smile at each other. "…I am going to sleep, it's been a day!"

"Okay son, I will see you in the morning." Shane and Stephanie embraced. Shane ran up the staircase. Stephanie went to her bedroom. She noticed that Henry wasn't in the bed. Stephanie came back to the great room and Henry was not there.

Stephanie and Henry lived on a cul-de-sac that has a beautiful landscaped path to a 2-mile pond,

Stephanie and Henry often walked around the pond or they sat on the dock watching the ducks and swans. Stephanie saw that the car was still in the garage when she and Shane came in, so she decided to walk down to the pond to see if Henry was there.

Stephanie walked to the end of the cul-de-sac, she could see Henry standing looking over the pond. Stephanie walked up behind Henry, "It's not worth jumping." That's what they would always say to the other when they would come to the pond.

Henry turned and smirked, "Tonight it sure does feel like it."
"Henry! I don't want to hear you talk like that. We have faced difficult times before and this is no different, this too shall pass."

Henry turned toward Stephanie, "You are showing such unconditional love and I am having difficulty receiving because I have been dishonest for so long. I have hurt you and Shane. It is one thing to have an affair, but to produce a child with your best friend is another matter. Stephanie, I wanted to tell you…."

Henry breaks down in tears leaning over the dock post.

"Henry, I already told you, we will get through this. I think after talking with Shane tonight he will be okay. You need to start working on mending your relationship with Carl."

"I think I am the last person he wants to hear from. You haven't even asked me when, why, or what I was thinking? You are simply amazing to me."

"Henry it's because I remember when, I can do the math sweetie…we almost didn't make it and I considered breaking covenant as well. Just as you and Jessica have always been able to talk, I have always been able to talk to Henry. He and I during that same time almost crossed the boundary, but we didn't."

"Stephanie, I am sorry I drove you to that, but I did cross the boundary," said Henry.

Stephanie put her arms around Henry, "You have to forgive yourself first, once you do that you can accept my forgiveness. Carl is going to schedule DNA testing."

"Thank you Stephanie, I couldn't ask for a better wife." Henry wrapped his arms around Stephanie. "How is Jill and what's happening to Jessica?"

"Stephanie began to cry, Jill bless her heart is so heartbroken, but Shane is comforting her and has faith. He told us tonight he doesn't believe that Jill is your daughter. He said in his spirit he doesn't believe she is. Jessica on the other hand has had a complete psychotic break down. Carl and I took her to Rose Farland Wellness Center. It will take some time for her to recover, it took this long for her to break down, recovery could…" Stephanie just cried as Henry and Stephanie held each other.

"I hate to hear that, it would have never come to this if Jessica and I didn't keep this secret, now look what is happening. A time in Shane and Jill's life that should be joyous and celebratory has been nothing but. Granny P dies, he finds out the love of his life is his sister that's too much for a seventeen year old young man."

Stephanie through her tears said, "Henry, Shane is much stronger and he is stronger in his faith than you think. I told you he believes he and Jill are not siblings and I choose to join my faith with his."

Chapter Twenty-five

Selma awoke with the warmth of the morning sun on her face; she reached for her pump to release the pain medication. She heard gagging in the bathroom. She called out in a minor panic, "Marcie! Marcie!" Marcie came out of the bathroom holding her stomach and slightly bent over. "Marcie, what happened to you? Did your father…." Selma began to cry, Marcie walked to her mother's bed,

"Mom I am fine. Nothing is broken, but you need to know I did file a report against Daddy. Mom, I

have suffered long enough and so have you…"
Marcie felt sick to her stomach and ran to the
bathroom. Selma could hear her gagging, but her
tear stricken face turned to a smile as Mark
Swindoll walked through the door.

"Good morning, Selma!"
"Good morning Mark, how are you?" Mark said,
"I am great now, how are you? Feeling any
better?"
 "I am still experiencing a great deal of pain, but I
am more worried about Marcie right now. She is
in the bathroom." Mark leaned over the bed to kiss
Selma on her forehead when Marcie came out the
bathroom, Mark turned as Marcie was about to
pass out. "Marcie!" Selma cried out. Mark ran to
Marcie's side. Selma hit the nurses call button.

"Yes, Mrs. Taylor" Selma called out, "Can
someone come and help my daughter, she just
passed out." "Someone is on the way, Mrs.
Taylor." The nurses ran to Marcie's aide. Mark

helped them get Marcie in the bed. Marcie came to. The nurse took Marcie's vitals and ordered saline solution for anti-dehydration.

"Marcie I will also have the lab come up and complete some more blood work to determine what is going on." Selma commented, "She was just in the bathroom regurgitating."

"Marcie, how long have you been doing that?" said the nurse. "Marcie replied, a couple times last night and twice this morning." Marcie noticed Mark by her bedside. "What are you doing here?"

Chapter Twenty-six

Stephanie was in the kitchen fixing breakfast. Egg, sausage, bacon and biscuits aroma filled the kitchen. Stephanie had the table prepared for her family. She was not expecting Henry to go to the office, or Shane to go to school due to the late night. Shane came down the steps vivaciously liberated.

"Good morning mother..." Shane was almost singing her name.
"Good morning son, I didn't expect you to leave the house this morning."

"I am going to grab some breakfast and pick up Jill, I talked to her this morning and I think that her lying around the house will not be good for her, so I am going to take the same advice."

"Alright then make her a breakfast sandwich when you fix yours."

"Ah, that sounds good. I will text her now."

"Where was Dad last night, when we came in? How is he doing?" said Shane.

"He is alright; he is dealing with a lot of shame and guilt. He is worried about you and Jill. I told him I have forgiven him, but he has to forgive himself first before he can accept anything from me or anyone else."

"Mom, I need to talk with him too, let him know I am alright also. Does he know Jill and I aren't siblings?"

"I told him, you are much stronger in your faith than he realizes. Shane, how will you feel if the DNA results return that your father is Jill's biological father?"

"Mom, I am not living in a fantasy world. I have already thought about it, but I am speaking what I desire in my heart. I prayed about this prior to saying anything to Jill. Mom, I don't think I missed it, she is my wife, and God wouldn't do that to me. He would not let Jill be my sister. I believe that all this is happening to try my faith."

"Son, I am so proud of you…"
"Mom, I am chip off the old block."
"The *old* block…I beg your pardon." Shane and Stephanie laughed. Shane grabbed his mother and picked her up swinging her around in the kitchen. "Put me down Shane!"

Shane finished making the breakfast sandwiches for him and Jill. The automatic timer on the coffee maker activated. Coffee along with the breakfast has now permeated throughout the house. Stephanie pulled out a nice gift bag for Shane to put the sandwiches in.

"Mom, I don't need this, a plastic bag will do."
"Shane, Shane, Shane, I have told you several times before… presentation is everything."

They both smiled. Stephanie continued, "I hope to know something about Granny P's funeral arrangements. You and Jill should get your assignments for the week, just in case."

"That's a good idea, especially with Aunt Jessica in the hospital. See you later mom. I am going to drive my car this morning."
"Love you Shane," said Stephanie.
"Love you too, Mom."

Shane walked out the garage door as Henry was entering the kitchen. "Good morning my lord…"

"Oh Stephanie, please you're killing me…."

"Look Henry McFinley. I am not going to allow you to wallow in self-pity, doubt, shame and grief. We have invested too much time in each other to give up now. We believe God for everything else in our lives, this situation didn't take God by surprise and if He is not surprised why should we. Draw on the Word of God that's on the inside of you. *His Grace is made perfect in our weakness.* I haven't given up on this marriage and neither will you! I am here Henry, I am here!"

Henry couldn't help but cry after Stephanie's speech, he knew she was right, but the guilt of it was still in the fore front of his mind. "Stephanie, I would be a fool to give up on us. I love you babe, thank you!" Stephanie smiles at Henry as she fixes his plate. I have all your favorites including cheese grits. Henry couldn't help but think that the pot of grits could potentially come flying his way, but instead Stephanie placed his plate on the table in front of him along with a jar of blackberry preserves from their favorite farmer's market.

"I am going to go to Marcie's school and get all of her work for the week and then I am going over to the hospital. Carl is setting up a DNA test. I will let you know when that is going to be."

"I am going to try and talk to Carl today."
"Well...I think that would be a good thing, I will give you a call later," said Stephanie. Stephanie grabbed her purse out of the family room, when the doorbell rang. Henry started to get up from his breakfast.

"No honey I will get it," said Stephanie. Stephanie looked through the peephole on the door and opened it. "Good morning Carl!" they both embraced.

"Is Henry up?"

"Yes, he is. Why don't you go in and join him for breakfast." Stephanie and Carl walked back to the kitchen after Carl secured the front door. "Look who's here," said Stephanie. "I will see you both later, behave and definitely don't tear up my house!"

Stephanie smirked trying to make light of a very tense situation. It didn't back fire, Henry replied. "Aw you got jokes."
"Yea, it appears she does," said Carl. Stephanie left out for the garage.

"Hey man, want some breakfast? Stephanie even fixed cheese grits," said Henry.

"I would thanks." Henry fixed a plate for Carl and sat it down in front of him. Stephanie had a pitcher of fresh squeezed orange juice on the table. There were a few moments of silence between Carl and Henry when finally they both began to apologize at the same time. Henry took the lead in the conversation.

"Man, I apologize. No matter what was going on with Stephanie and me. I didn't have the right…" Carl interrupted, "No you didn't, but we have to get past that because what's done is done. It takes two to tango and Jessica is just as much at fault as you are. I am more concerned about Jill at this point. I am expecting to have DNA testing scheduled today and we should have results within the week. I was so mad at you and thought how could you do this to me? But, Stephanie brought me down off my self-righteous horse when she reminded me that we almost crossed that line around the same time."

"Yea, Stephanie told me about it," said Henry. "Henry, she is an incredible woman and you would have been a fool to leave her," said Carl. Henry agreed.

"I am not here to reassure you that our relationship will return to what it was. I think I still need some time. With Jessica not well and Jill suddenly questioning where she belongs, they will both be my priority. I have reassured Jill that no matter what the test results yield she will always be my baby girl. I don't want you to interfere with that. She may want a different relationship with you….more of a father relationship with you, which I am going to tell you if she does, it will be difficult for me to handle. I have raised her as my own and I want you to remember and respect the fact that she is mine. Do you understand where I am coming from?" Carl was not nasty with Henry but he was very matter of fact and firm.

Henry replied, "I believe that after all of these years, I have played a second father to Jill having believed that she could be my daughter. We were never tested. I just believed Jessica when she was carrying Jill; she thought it was my baby and not yours. You were both on the mend and she asked that I would allow the two of you to raise Jill as your own. I agreed to that for obvious reasons. I completely understand where you are and I didn't expect for our relationship to go back to the way things were. You do need to know that I wanted to tell you and Stephanie so many times. I just conceded to Jessica…I should have insisted."

Carl's cell phone rings and he takes the call in the next room. Carl returns and announces to Henry. "Our testing will take place this afternoon at 4:00 p.m."

"I will let Stephanie and Shane know. Do you think that we can agree to read the results together, for Shane and Jill's sake?" said Henry.

Carl sat at the table tossing through the food on his plate that he barely ate, pondering Henry's question. "I will ask Jill how she feels about that and whatever she would like to do, I will agree to that."

Henry agreed with Carl. "I am going to get out of here, please enjoy the rest of your breakfast," said Carl.

Henry got up and walked Carl to the front door. Henry said, "Carl…." Carl turned and looked at Henry; he knew Henry was nervous the whole time they were talking. Henry was sweating and his silk pajamas were sticking to his body. Carl could see that through his matching silk robe. Henry continued, "…I just wanted to say…uhm, thanks for coming over…uhm…I am so sorry man. You have to know I am really sorry, for breaking your trust and the deceit was all just uncalled for. I risked everything between you and me. The years of friendship…I love you man, know that hasn't changed."

Carl nodded his head and said, "I know Henry. I know."

Chapter Twenty-seven

The state trooper is proceeding down highway A8 when he spots a Mercedes E-320 that has been hair pinned between two trees. The trooper gets close enough to call in the license plate, and then gets out with his hand on his gun, to investigate if there are any survivors. He can see the driver pinned in the car. He phones back to dispatch to have paramedics dispatched immediately along with the *Jaws of Life* to get the driver out. He checks for a pulse, which is barely felt.

The trooper calls back, "The driver barely has a pulse…" The dispatcher tells the trooper that the car is registered to *"…one Calvin Taylor who is wanted for questioning in a rape case."*

The trooper replies, "I have no way of identifying the driver. He is not responding to voice commands." Sirens can be heard coming down the highway. Moans and a faint cry for help from the car permeate the air.

Chapter Twenty-eight

Stephanie arrives at North General after leaving Marcie's school. Stephanie has been on the phone trying to determine what the funeral arrangements are going to be for Granny P. She did learn from Pastor's secretary that Granny P's niece flew in from Germany to take care of her aunt's arrangements.

The phone rang, "Hello...hi honey. I am at the hospital, how did things go with Carl? I see four o'clock... I will call Shane and leave him a message. I love you Henry, okay, bye."

Stephanie proceeds to Marcie's room. She calls Shane and leaves a message for him to come straight home after school; they will ride together for the testing.

Stephanie reaches the elevator and rides to Selma's floor. She makes her greetings to the nurses at their station. When Stephanie walks into Selma's room, she is surprised to see Marcie in a hospital bed and more surprise to see Mark Swindoll.

"Hello everyone," said Stephanie. As everyone returned their greetings, she immediately noticed Marcie's bruises and scares. "Marcie what happened? Are you okay?"

"Hi, Mrs. McFinley, I am not feeling my best, this morning, but all is well with me. I have never felt such liberation as I do now," said Marcie.

Mark Swindoll said, "I just wanted to check on Selma and Marcie and also let you know about Mrs. Perry?" "What happened to Mrs. Perry," said Selma.

"She was rushed into the hospital the same night you were and she didn't make it," said Mark.

"Yes, we are awaiting funeral arrangement now," said Stephanie. Marcie began to cry, Stephanie went to her side.

Mark said, "I will let you ladies have your time alone. I will check back a little later." Mark walked out the room.

Stephanie said to Selma, "How are you feeling this morning Selma?"

Selma through her tears said, "Stephanie this has all been too much. A man that I have given my life for…has done nothing but break my heart, beat me silly and furthermore he has…has…"

Selma just broke down; Marcie moved slowly out of her bed and moved her IV near her mother's bed to try to console her.

"Mom, I told you. I am alright. Everything is going to be alright." Marcie tried to hold her mother as close as possible, with their hospital equipment confining them.

Stephanie's phone rang she forgot to turn it off in the lobby. She took the call closer to the bathroom. "That was Pastor's secretary, Granny P's funeral is going to be next Tuesday," said Stephanie.

Marcie and Selma barely acknowledge Stephanie's announcement. Stephanie wanted to stay with Selma and Marcie but did not want to intrude. They appeared to need some time alone to talk. Whatever happened to Marcie, Stephanie knew Cal Taylor was behind it all.

Stephanie said, "Is there anything else I can do for either of you? Marcie, I have a weeks' worth of work for you on the table there. Do you want me to get anything? Henry and I can go by the house."

Selma interrupted, "NO! Don't risk it. We will be fine. Calvin could be there."

"If Dad went back to the house, he has been arrested," Marcie said with confidence.

"Marcie, you had your father arrested?" said Selma. "Mom I told you, enough is enough. I have had enough."

Marcie started back to her bed when she asked Stephanie to get the trashcan for her. Marcie threw the little bit of breakfast she had tried to eat.

"Marcie you need to sit down, we need to know why you keep regurgitating?" said Selma.

"How long has this been going on," said Stephanie

"Since last night," said Marcie.

Stephanie had a very strange feeling when Courtney walked in. Courtney was not her typical perky self. Marcie on the other hand was very perky.

"Good morning Courtney, how are you?"
"Good morning everyone, Mrs. Taylor, Mrs. McFinley, Marcie...Mrs. McFinley can I speak with Mrs. Taylor and Marcie alone please."

"Oh, oh sure, I will actually come back a little later, maybe I will call to check on you both. If you need anything, anything at all, please do not hesitate to call me," said Stephanie.

"Thank you Stephanie and thanks for picking up Marcie's work," said Selma. Stephanie walked out of the room.

"Courtney what do you need to discuss with us," said Selma. Courtney pulled up a chair between the two beds and looked down at the floor almost the entire time. "I wanted to let you know about...uhm...Marcie's blood test. The results have come back...and...uhm...there is no way to say this but to just say it. Marcie, you are pregnant."

Selma Taylor screamed to the top of her lungs. Courtney anticipated the response and asked a nurse to be on standby with a sedative. Marcie on the other hand was extremely calm and laid back in the bed and said, "God is still in control."

Chapter Twenty-nine

One Week Later

Henry and Stephanie were at the gravesite of
Granny P along with Carl, Shane and Jill. The
funeral was a home going like no other. They all
learned of Granny's fame in the musical world.
Several famous names of that time were present,
with selections from quartets and a special tribute
from a woman who credits Granny P with her
interest in playing the harp. Her tribute of *"It Is*

Well with My Soul" left everyone in the church in tears. Shane and Jill continued to comfort one another at Granny P's gravesite. At the conclusion, Shane took a rose from Granny's coffin spray of flowers and gave it to Jill. Jill smelled the rose and continued to cry.

Granny P's niece came over to the McFinleys and Richardsons. "Thank you so much for all that you have done for Aunt Gertrude. She loved Shane and Jill and often talked about you. It was nice meeting you both."

As the crowd was dismissing and going to their respective cars, Carl walked over to Henry. "Did you bring your letter?"
Henry replied, "Yes and as I agreed we will read and discuss it with Shane and Jill together."
Carl said, "Where do you all want to go?" Shane and Jill walked up during the conversation.

Shane said, "If no one objects, let's do it right here." Henry said, "Shane this is really not the appropriate place, we will need to sit and talk."

Carl agreed, "Yes, we could go to a restaurant or to the park around the corner." "Shane said, "No, there are benches right there, let's get this over with. This is an appropriate place because regardless of the outcome everything dies here, let's bury it here."

Jill boldly agreed. "Daddy this will be fine." Henry and Carl still tried to get them to reconsider. Shane bluntly said, "Read it here! Everything dies and we bury today....RIGHT NOW!"

Stephanie began to walk toward the benches hoping Henry and Carl would follow. Shane and Jill walked hand and hand behind Stephanie. Henry and Carl turned and looked at each other. "That boy of yours is something else Henry."

"I know Carl, I know." Shane and Jill sit on the bench. Stephanie sits on the other side of Shane trying to hold both him and Jill.

It was a beautiful day outside. The wind was gently blowing. The fragrance of fresh flowers on the local gravesites permeates as the wind blew. There appeared to be so much life in this place of death. The birds chirping and the green grass perfectly groomed. Carl and Henry pulled the letters out of their inside pockets. They both looked at each other and proceeded to open the letters. Shane held Jill's hand tightly; he could feel her body shaking all over.

Carl and Henry opened their letters at the same time. They read over their letters; Carl fell to his knees with the letter over his face.

Thank you for purchasing this dynamic book
"Covenant of Lies The Revealed Truth"
By Holly Spence.

Pre-Order the sequel of
"Covenant of Lies the Healing Truth" at
www.monarchpublicationsllc.webs.com.

Purchase the first book in the series
"Covenant of Lies the Revealed Truth"
See what others are saying about

"I really enjoyed the book and read it the same night I purchased it. Once I started reading I couldn't stop because I had to know what happened next. It was exciting and emotional and I can't wait for the sequel!"
                                                    T Smoot

"...sometime when you start to read a book, you can not get into it for the first two or three chapters. Then as I was reading I thought, do I know these people? This is like church folks, we have to go eat somewhere after church. Then as I read on this is everyday life. People in the church are losing jobs, hurting, and hiding the pain. The lies need to be exposed. I was not expecting Jill and Shawn were sister and brother. And the way you stop it..."
                                                    A. Morris

"The book was a roller coaster ride of emotions. Full of suspense, laughs, tears and pure joy. The story lines are believable and the characters seemed to be living their lives in front of your very eyes... Their life fuelled by the affects of lust and deception certainly keeps your attention. The life lessons they will have to endure are the ones that will destroy or strengthen families and friendships. Boundaries are definitely crossed and how these families survive will be testaments of their faith....Hurry with part two, your fans are waiting..."

M. Moore

CONVENANT OF LIES THE UNTOLD TRUTH is a quick read, a page turner with a lot of substance. The plot development is full of characters' situations and turning points that ends with a dual climax. This book hold its literary merit as good fiction by allowing the reader to delve into the story line with tension/ release patterns and vivid image formation. Christian lives and values are on display in full spectrum in this debut fictional novel by Holly Spence.

Anita M. Boclair,
Founder BRANCHES (Boclair's Reading Association – Nurturing Change, Healing, Empowerment & Satisfaction)

"Holly...your book is filled with drama and excitement at every turn. The characters leave the imagination open to anything. I actually feel like I know them."

Authoress Valerie Brown
Flowing In The
Spirit

"Equally riveting and disturbing, Covenant Of Lies is a titillating read. In it, author Holly Spence takes four average, everyday individuals with whom readers will easily relate and thrusts them into the middle of self-created storms of turmoil and heartache. Some of the decisions that Carl, Henry, Jessica, and Stephanie ultimately make may be deplorable, but they are no different than the impulse moves made by millions of people all over the world every day. As such, Spence's tale inspires more empathy than judgmental wrath, ultimately encouraging the reader to think twice before succumbing to the lures of temptation - not tomention the false promises of the flesh. Timely and eye-opening, Covenant Of Lies is a solid debut from a promising new literary voice."

Apex Reviews
www.apexreviews.net
info@apexreviews.net

"Covenant Of Lies is a 5 star Read"

"In this novel, author Holly Spence tells the story of everyday individuals and the problems and heartache they encounter. The situations that the characters find themselves in are unimaginable, but believable and real. Some may find themselves judging the characters while others may sympathize. In any case it tugs at your emotions and causes one to really ponder the consequences of following temptation."

Karen Brown
Author "Control Issues"
www.klynnbrownpublishing.com

"A Definite Page Turner"

"I have not read a book in two days since I was fifteen and I was reading Archie Books! This was such an interesting read! Holly Spence has a knack for holding the attention of her audience. Lots of twists and turns; I love a suspenseful novel! Ms. Spence, looking forward to the sequel!"

Rebecca C. Greene
Author of "Sisters in the Name of Love" and
"Diary 15" series
www.rebeccasbooks.com

See additional books by author Holly Spence

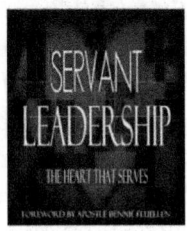

See what others are saying about this dynamic

publication;

"The heart issues that you describe are right on...All servants, even those who are leaders can benefit from preparing a heart to serve."

Dr. Rodney Swope
Rod & Staff Enterprises
www.rodnstaff.net

"We often need a goad to cause us to stop and take the time to reaffirm our commitment to Christ and service others as an outflow of that commitment. This book offers good biblical and comical anecdotes to cause us to pause in our journey reflect and readjust our hearts."

Elder Monica Keenon
iSucseed, LLC
isucseed@hotmail.com

"Servant Leadership The Heart That Serves" is also available on a 2-CD audio disc.

 **Disc 1**

 **Disc 2**

Servant Leadership is available for corporate bible studies and may be purchased in bulk please contact Monarch Publications, LLC at monarchpublicationsllc@yahoo.com

You've rendered an excellent program of empowerment. Very nicely done! Good flow. Nice overlaps between key topics. I especially liked the areas where you completely turn loose and throw the fire of your personality into it. That fire is "you" and makes the book. Very impressive methodology. Keep it up!

Larry Trujillo
Principal Consultant
Oracle Corporation

I think your book so far is well laid out, easy to read, interactive and engaging. Each chapter I've read, entices me to participate in the process and the activities. It's very applicable to life, not just work.

Cindy Dutra
Oracle Corporation

Well I have a 2-year-old son and a 3.5-year-old daughter and even though they are not in school, I still run around like a chicken with my head cut off. Sometimes you have to take 10 minutes to just calm down, but sometimes Holly it's not possible. I always worked a 9 to 5 or 9 to 8 before I had kids. I'm trying to get this online business situated plus my own business situated so I will have more than 10 minutes to relax. I've seen it done and I see it being done. You know what my 10 minutes consist of? Giving back whether it be advice, whether it just be thanking God for all he has done for me and people who've I've come in contact with. Even though I don't lay my head to rest until 11 sometimes 12, I still feel my mind working. But you have given me something to think about. RELAX, RELATE, RELEASE!

Annie McCall

Workshops are currently being scheduled for corporate entry-level management, senior executives, church leadership and team workshops.

For workshop information and speaking engagement, requests please send an email to monarchpublcaitonsllc@yahoo.com

Appendix

[i] It Is Well Will My Soul by Horatio G Spafford, 1873
Copyright: Public Domain